This **Chicken House** book

belongs to

....

....

For Lindsey, with love and thanks — LR
For Lily, Florence and Albie with love from Marg — MC

© 2008 The Chicken House

First published in the United Kingdom in 2008 by
The Chicken House, 2 Palmer Street, Frome, Somerset, BA11 1DS
www.doublecluck.com

Text © 2008 Lynne Rickards
Illustrations © 2008 Margaret Chamberlain

Designed by Ian Butterworth

Printed and bound in Singapore by Imago

3 5 7 9 10 8 6 4

British Library Cataloguing in Publication Data available
Library of Congress Cataloguing in Publication data available

HB ISBN: 978-1-905294-73-2
PB ISBN: 978-1-905294-74-9

Pink!

by Lynne Rickards

illustrated by Margaret Chamberlain

Chicken House

One sunny morning, Patrick woke up to find he had turned bright

PINK!

His beak was pink, his flippers were pink — he was pink from head to foot.

'This is terrible!' cried Patrick. 'What will all my friends say? Whoever heard of a PINK penguin?'

Patrick looked. He saw hundreds of beautiful birds.
'Are some of them boys?' asked Patrick as he gazed at the picture.
'At least half of them,' laughed his dad. 'You see? Boys can be pink!'

Patrick got teased at school for being pink.
  'Don't worry, they'll get used to it soon enough,'
said his mum. Patrick wasn't so sure. He didn't
like being different from everyone else.

One Saturday morning Patrick pulled out his rucksack. He put in his pyjamas and his favourite soft toy.

'I don't fit in here any more,' he told his mum and dad. 'I'm going to Africa to see those flamingos.'

Patrick went to the water's edge. Africa was a long way north, but he was a strong swimmer. He swam for seven days and seven nights.

When the water began to feel warmer, he knew he was nearly there.

On the eighth day Patrick arrived in a wide bay. On the shore he saw hundreds of flamingos, just like in the picture! He waddled up to them and held out a pink flipper. 'How do you do?' he said politely.

The flamingos looked down at him curiously. They had long necks and spindly legs and were very, very tall. 'Will you join us for lunch?' one of them asked Patrick. 'Oh, yes, thank you!' he cried.

All the flamingos dipped their long, curvy beaks into the water and began skimming them back and forth. Patrick's beak was quite the wrong shape, so he came up coughing and spluttering. Poor Patrick would have to go hungry!

After lunch the flamingos had a nap.
They all stood on one leg and tucked their heads down.

Patrick tried to stand on one leg too. He was hopeless!

When sunset came, it was time to fly to the nesting ground. The flamingos flapped their wings and rose into the air like a big pink cloud.

One small, pink penguin was left behind.

'This is no good,' said Patrick. He didn't belong here, even though he was pink. It was time to go home.

The next morning Patrick set off.
He swam for seven days and seven nights,
until the water felt lovely and cold again.

Patrick's mum and dad were very pleased to see him. 'You must have missed your favourite breakfast,' said Dad. 'I sure did!' said Patrick with his mouth full.

When Patrick went back to school, his whole class crowded around him.
'Where have you been, Patrick?' they asked. 'We missed you!'

Patrick's teacher asked him to give a little talk about his travels.
He stood at the front of the class with a big map and a pointer.

'I went to Africa,' Patrick told his friends.

'Wow, you swam all that way?' asked Billy. Patrick nodded proudly.

'In Africa the water is warm,' he continued. 'There are colourful fish, and tall pink birds called flamingos that stand on one leg.'

'Did you see one of those?' asked Lulu.

'I saw hundreds!' answered Patrick. 'They were beautiful. But you know, they can't swim underwater or slide on their tummies like we can.'

'Really?' said his classmates.
'What a shame!'

After school, Patrick waddled home with his best friend Arthur.
'You know, Arthur,' said Patrick, 'I'm really glad I went to Africa.'
'I'm really glad you came back!' said Arthur.

'Me too!' laughed Patrick.
'Penguins belong at the South Pole.
Even pink penguins.'
'Especially pink penguins!'
said Arthur happily.

That night at bedtime, Patrick said,
'You were right, Mum.
Nobody teases me any more.'
He snuggled down and smiled.
Being different wasn't so bad after all.